D1077786

The Old Tree Stories

Boastful Mr Bear

First published in Great Britain in 1989 by
Belitha Press Limited
31 Newington Green, London N16 9PU
Text and illustrations in this format © Belitha Press 1989
Text and illustrations copyright © Peter Firmin 1989

Printed in Hong Kong for Imago Publishing

British Library Cataloguing in Publication Data
Firmin, Peter
  Boastful Mr. Bear.
  I. Title   II. Series
  823′.914[J]

ISBN 0-947553-01-0

PETER FIRMIN

The Old Tree Stories

Boastful Mr Bear

🌼 Belitha Press

Mr Bear stood at the bottom of
the Old Tree.
He banged the tree with a stick
just to show how big he was.

He said: "I'm the biggest and the best, and I'm going to build a hut."

He beat down the weeds with a stick.
He cleared a space for his hut.
"I'll help you with that job,"
said Mr Fox. "I'll help you
to clear the weeds."

"I'm the biggest and the best, I
can do it by myself," said Mr Bear.
"I don't need your help."
Mr Fox climbed over the fence
to be out of the way of the bear.

Mr Bear stamped around the Old Tree
to smooth the ground for his hut.
"I could help you with that little job,"
said Master Hare. "I could
help you to stamp the ground."
"I'm the biggest and the best,
I can do it by myself," said Mr Bear.

He thumped and bumped on the ground.
"I don't need your help."

Mr Bear gathered sticks and logs
of wood to build his hut.
"I'll help you with that little job,"
said Miss Crow. "I could help you
to gather sticks."

"I'm the biggest and best,
I can do it by myself,"
said Mr Bear. He heaved a
big log of wood on the heap.
"I don't need your help. So
why don't you leave me alone!"

Mr Bear soon built his hut.
The hut had walls of wood
and a roof of sticks.
It was a very good hut for a bear.
He was pleased with it.

Mr Bear collected corn and
berries and sweet wild apples
to eat in the winter.
"I'll help you with that little
job," said Miss Mouse. "I could
help you to collect food."

"I'm the biggest and you are the smallest in the wood," said Mr Bear. "I certainly don't need your help! So just keep out of my way."

Mr Bear danced round his hut.
"I've made a fine hut, and I've
plenty of food, and I did it all
by myself," he boasted.
"I don't need anyone's help."

Mr Bear tripped over a root of the
Old Tree . . . He fell over backwards,
into the bushes . . . He sat in the
middle of a blackthorn bush!

"Ouch!" he cried. "There's a thorn
in my tail!"

Mr Bear reached to pull out
the thorn.
He twisted
and turned.
OUCH!

He wriggled
and struggled.
OUCH!
That thorn
really hurt.

But Mr Bear could not quite reach it.
He needed some help.

"Let me help you," said Miss Rat.
"I could pull out that thorn."
"I'd be glad if you would," said Mr Bear.
So Miss Rat pulled out the thorn.
"That's much better," said Mr Bear.
"Thank you . . .

"Isn't it good to have friends."